George Ticknor Curtis

The Just Supremacy of Congress over the Territories

SALZWASSER
VERLAG

George Ticknor Curtis

The Just Supremacy of Congress over the Territories

Reprint of the original, first published in 1859.

1st Edition 2022 | ISBN: 978-3-37513-220-0

Verlag (Publisher): Salzwasser Verlag GmbH, Zeilweg 44, 60439 Frankfurt, Deutschland
Vertretungsberechtigt (Authorized to represent): E. Roepke, Zeilweg 44, 60439 Frankfurt, Deutschland
Druck (Print): Books on Demand GmbH, In de Tarpen 42, 22848 Norderstedt, Deutschland

THE

JUST SUPREMACY OF CONGRESS

OVER

THE TERRITORIES.

––––––

BY GEORGE TICKNOR CURTIS.

––––––

SUPER ANTIQUAS VIAS.

BOSTON:

A. WILLIAMS AND COMPANY,

100, WASHINGTON STREET.

1859.

INTRODUCTORY NOTE.

IT is, perhaps, scarcely necessary to say, that this pamphlet was written as an answer to the article by the Hon. STEPHEN A. DOUGLAS, which originally appeared in Harpers' Magazine, entitled " The Dividing Line between Federal and Local Authority; Popular Sovereignty in the Territories;" and which has since been re-published in a separate form. Private engagements and other circumstances have delayed the publication of my Essay longer than I had originally intended; but I believe that the subject is not likely to lose its interest. The impersonal style in which it is written is to be accounted for by the fact that it was designed for publication in some periodical work, and it was not convenient to make any change in this respect after I determined to publish it in a pamphlet. I should add, that I have seen no other of Mr. Douglas's writings on this subject than the article to which this pamphlet undertakes to reply; nor have I read the papers written by the Attorney-General, Mr. Black.

G. T. C.

BOSTON, Nov. 5, 1859.

BOSTON:

PRINTED BY JOHN WILSON AND SON,

22, SCHOOL STREET.

JUST SUPREMACY OF CONGRESS

OVER THE TERRITORIES.

THE appearance, in a popular magazine, of an article on a constitutional question, written by a prominent candidate for the Presidency, with his name prefixed to it, is something new. We do not know that there can be any reasonable objection to this mode of promulgating or defending political opinions. It has one advantage over electioneering speeches, inasmuch as what is written is likely to be more deliberate than what is spoken; and if our public men would employ the pen a little more, and the tongue a little less, we think that they and the country would be gainers. On the other hand, what is thus carefully prepared in an elaborate article, as the doctrine on which a statesman means to challenge the suffrages of his countrymen for the highest office in their gift, brings him in a peculiarly responsible attitude before the tribunals of contemporary criticism and public judgment. What he says and maintains in such a form is not like a Congressional speech, which may be thrown off in the heat of debate or while defending or attacking a particular measure, and which is liable, even if not likely, to be forgotten when the interest in the occasion has passed. Mr. Douglas steps forward boldly and frankly, as becomes him, and puts on record, in a journal of a very wide circulation, his opinions upon a grave constitutional question, which enters largely into the politics of the day; and the doctrine which he thus promulgates is notoriously relied upon by his friends, as the great topic, the championship of which is to carry him into the White House. He certainly will not be disposed to complain if his opinions thus put forth are subjected to examination in the same form of discussion.

We shall begin what we have to say upon this subject with the free admission, that there are a good many elements of popularity both in Mr. Douglas's character and in his present position. The public man who presents himself as an advocate for the right of self-government for any people, however they are situated, will always command popular sympathy in this country. But we are not now concerned with Mr. Douglas's chances or means of political success, but with the soundness and correctness of his constitutional opinions. Whether he is or is not of that order of men who "would rather be right than be President," we do not presume to decide ; but we are sure for ourselves, that, having no personal interest in the matter, we would rather be right than be able to prevent him or any other man from reaching the Presidency, if we had the power of all the nominating conventions or of all the voters in the land.

It is the purpose of Mr. Douglas's article to maintain, that the people of a Territory have the right to decide, independently of the will of Congress, whether the institution of slavery shall or shall not exist among them while they are in the Territorial condition. On a cursory reading of his paper, we were a little at a loss to determine whether he meant to be understood that this power belongs to the people of a Territory because the organic act bestows upon them general legislative power, or, as in the case of Kansas, declares that they shall be free to form their own institutions in their own way ; or whether he holds that the people of a Territory are originally free to establish or prohibit slavery without any Congressional declaration or-grant of such a power, or even against a Congressional prohibition. But, on a more careful perusal, we find that his argument goes the entire length of maintaining, that, in reference to what he calls their local concerns and internal polity, the people of a Territory are absolutely sovereign in the same sense in which the people of a State are sovereign. In order to establish what he calls "popular sovereignty in the Territories," Mr. Douglas undertakes to define the dividing line between federal and local authority ; and he places it, in respect to the Territories, substantially where it is in respect to the States. He sums up the whole discussion in the following "principle," — "that every distinct political community, loyal to the Constitution and the Union, is *entitled* to all the rights, privileges, and immunities of self-government in respect to their local concerns and internal polity, subject only to the Constitution of the United States."

A very important question, therefore, arises upon Mr. Douglas's proposition ; namely, What does he mean when he says that the people of a Territory are "entitled" to all the rights of self-government ? Are they "entitled" morally, or legally ? as a matter of comity, or as a strict constitutional right ? If Mr. Douglas were asked this question as a jurist, in a matter of private right involving a correct answer to it, would any man be disposed to risk a litigation upon the correctness of the views by which Mr. Douglas undertakes to guide and enlighten the political opinions of his countrymen ? In our judgment, the dividing line between federal and local authority, in respect to the Territories, would have to be drawn more in accordance with settled principles than it is drawn by him, before it would be safe to admit the soundness of his very sweeping conclusion.

Nor is he any more satisfactory to us as a statesman than he would be as a jurisconsult. The importance of a clear and reliable answer to the question, "In what sense and how are the people of a Territory *entitled* to the full and absolute right of self-government ?" will be apparent to any one who will consider that polygamy is an institution which must be within this right, if the right exists in the unqualified extent for which Mr. Douglas claims it. This, and a variety of other institutions which might be against the will of Congress and the entire policy of a Christian civilization, would come within his principle. The vast inconvenience of his doctrine, therefore, renders it in the highest degree necessary to ascertain where his opinions, if they are to become predominant in our government, are to lead us ; for if it be true, as he seems to us to maintain, that the mere fact of their organization into a distinct political community entitles the people of one of the Territories of the United States, before they are admitted as a sovereign State of this Union, to make what laws or institutions they see fit, upon the plea that such laws or institutions relate to their internal concerns, it is quite essential to our peace and safety to know whether they are so "entitled" in a moral sense only, or in a strict constitutional and legal sense. If it is only as a moral claim that we are to regard the alleged right, then, in each particular case, Congress can consider the expediency of yielding what is demanded. If, on the other hand, the right is a constitutional and legal one, Congress can exercise no volition in the matter. Still, it occurs to us to ask, if the latter is the true character of the supposed right, what was the necessity and what is the meaning of Mr. Douglas's grant, made in his own Kansas-Nebraska Act to the people of those Territories, of " perfect freedom to form and regulate their domestic institutions in their own way"? Why repeal the Missouri Compromise, and enact the principle of " non-intervention" by Congress, if the people of a Territory, after they are made a Territory, are " entitled" to say that Congress shall not " intervene" in respect to their domestic institutions?

But it is not our purpose to anticipate the course of Mr. Douglas's argument. We shall endeavor to state and to answer it fairly, and shall then suggest what seem to us to be the insuperable difficulties which surround it.

The first part of Mr. Douglas's paper is occupied with a statement that the American Colonies, in their struggle with Great Britain, placed themselves upon the assertion of a right to legislate in their Colonial Assemblies respecting their local concerns, free from all interference by the English Parliament. The use which he makes of this is sufficiently apparent from his proposition, that " the dividing line between federal and local authority was familiar to the framers of the Constitution" [of the United States], because they had had a controversy with their mother-country respecting the dividing line between the authority of Parliament and the authority of their Colonial Legislatures. Nothing can be more inaccurate than the idea of an analogy between the question which our fathers raised with the Imperial Government, and the question, under the Constitution of the United States, respecting the power of Congress over the Territories. In the first place, we are to remember that it was no easy matter, even for Englishmen of liberal principles of government and with just feelings towards their American brethren, to state what the true theory of the English Constitution then was on the subject of the right of Parliament to bind the Colonies. Lord Chatham, it is true, in one of the most magnificent periods ever uttered in St. Stephen's, undertook a distinction between the regulation of trade and the levying of taxes ; and, in his haughty and daring dogmatism, he went so far as to assert that "there is no such thing, no such idea, in this Constitution, as a supreme power operating upon property." Burke, on the contrary, refused to discuss the *right* of Parliament to bind the Colonies, in respect either to trade or to taxation. He regarded the abstract merits of the dispute as —

> " That great Serbonian bog,
> Betwixt Damiata and Mount Cassius old,
> Where armies whole have sunk ; " —

and he bent the whole force of his splendid genius to the argument, that any exercise of the right, or attempt to exercise it, was inexpedient and dangerous. There is as little in the views maintained, in that controversy, on our side of the water, that can furnish a useful analogy, or aid us in determining what is the true relation of our Federal Government to those creatures of its legislation which we call the Territories. In the early stages of their contest with England, the people of the Colonies relied upon their charters and fundamental grants of political power, as so many assurances and guaranties of a limited right of independent local legislation. At a later period, when the contest grew closer, but when it was still necessary to secure a reconciliation if possible, they conceded the right of Parliament to bind them in matters of trade, but denied it in taxation. Soon, however, all consideration of their rights as British subjects, whether under charters or under the general principles of the Constitution of the Empire, was merged in the grand natural right of revolution, on which they constructed their " dividing line " between imperial and local authority. A triumphant Revolution, and an abrogation of all political power save their own, put an end to all disputes about their rights as subordinate or dependent communities. This portion of our history, therefore, can afford very little aid in drawing " the dividing line between federal and local authority " under a Constitution which no one has yet, happily, found it necessary to subject to any revolutionary process, but which all parties, by whatever name they are known, must administer upon rules that are consistent with the preservation of its just authority. The Constitution of the United States was not made for the purpose of embodying the principles of the Revolution. It was made in order that the fruits of that Revolution — the national independence — might not be lost in a state of anarchy, or in the tyranny to which anarchy inevitably tends. It was made in order that a regulated, republican liberty, founded upon order and system and positive institution, might save us from the domination of mobs, and from their natural consequence, — the oppression of military despotism.

The next step in Mr. Douglas's argument for " popular sovereignty in the Territories " is taken upon the action of Congress, before the Constitution was adopted, respecting the North-Western Territory ceded by Virginia to the Union ; and, strange to say, he confines his survey of this part of his subject to Mr. Jefferson's measure for the government of the Territory, which was adopted in 1784. He is quite correct in saying that this Jeffersonian plan of government for the tracts of country ceded, or to be ceded, to the Union by the States, contemplated the formation of political communities which it denominated " new States ; " that these " new States " were to be, in general, the same kind of communities as those which we now call " Territories ; " that they were to have temporary governments, on which was to be conferred a general power of legislation ; and that these governments were to remain until the communities should become States proper by admission into the Union. But, as to all the residue of the legislation which preceded the Constitution, Mr. Douglas is wholly silent. He represents Mr. Jefferson's plan as standing on the statute-book, " unrepealed and irrepealable," when the Convention assembled to form the Constitution. He omits to notice the Ordinance for the government of the North-Western Territory, adopted by Congress July 13, 1787, while the Federal Convention was sitting, and which was actually communicated to the Convention ; and, insisting that Mr. Jefferson's plan still stood as the existing law when the Constitution was framed, he makes the bold assertion, that the dividing line between federal and local authority was known to the framers of the Constitution, as a line which excluded from the power of the Federal Union all legislation respecting the internal concerns of Territories. This is not creditable to a person of Mr. Douglas's distinction. The simple truth is, that Mr. Jefferson's plan never took effect so far as to have a " new State " or Territorial government, of the kind contemplated, formed under it ; that the Ordinance of July 13, 1787, was framed to supersede, and actually repealed it, in reference to the North-Western Territory; that this Ordinance made numerous, and in some cases very strict, fundamental provisions concerning personal rights and relations, one of which related to slavery; that it was before the framers of the Constitution when they made the so-called Territorial clause, and when they passed the Constitution through its final draught; and consequently there is the strongest reason to contend, that " the dividing line between federal and local authority " in respect to Territories, as it had been practically drawn by the existing Congress, and as it was repeated by the Congress which, under the Constitution, afterwards re-enacted the Ordinance, was understood, in those days, as a line which included in the federal power any and all direct legislation, upon personal rights and relations, in such Territories, which it might be the pleasure of Congress to exercise.

Stepping over this great *hiatus* which Mr. Douglas has made in our national history, we come to the following singular proposition: —

"In the formation of the Constitution of the United States, the Federal Convention took the British Constitution, as interpreted and explained by the Colonies during their controversy with Great Britain, for their model; making such modifications in its structure and principles as the change in our condition had rendered necessary."

After running out what he considers the parallel between the two governments, and suggesting the views which our fathers maintained concerning the true relations of the mother-country to the Colonies, he asks if the framers of the Constitution can be supposed to have conferred upon Congress "that unlimited and despotic power over the people of the Territories which they had resisted with their blood when claimed by the British Parliament over British Colonies in America." This is somewhat *ad captandum*, and we doubt not Brother Jonathan will be struck with its force. But we believe it to be entirely unsound.

Probably Mr. Douglas stands alone in making the assertion, that the Constitution of the United States was *modelled* on the Constitution of Great Britain, as the latter was understood either by the colonists or by any one else. It has sometimes been charged as a reproach, that certain members of the Federal Convention leaned too much in their plans and wishes towards the English Constitution; but it has never been said before, so far as we know, that the whole body regarded that Constitution as their "model." Certainly it would not be difficult to show that the copy has so far departed from the "model," that very little resemblance can be detected. But suppose

until recently, been supposed to have plainly resided, so far as it required a positive text, is the clause known as the Territorial clause : —

" Congress shall have power to dispose of and make all needful rules and regulations respecting the Territory or other property belonging to the United States." (Art. iv. sect. 3.)

Mr. Douglas dismisses this source of power with the mere assumption, that " Territory " means, in this clause, nothing but landed property ; which meaning he rests upon the assertion, that, at the time when the Constitution was formed, the word " Territory " had " never been used or understood to designate a political community or government of any kind, in any law, compact, deed of cession, or public document." In this, we think, he is entirely mistaken. The very first clause in the Ordinance of 1787 ordains " that the said Territory, for the purposes of temporary government, be one district; subject, however, to be divided into two districts," &c. ; and these words " Territory " and " district " are used throughout the Ordinance as convertible terms, describing the *political community* for which the Ordinance makes certain provisions of fundamental law. Aside from this verbal criticism, however, Mr. Douglas surely does not require to be informed that the history and surrounding facts relating to this clause of the Constitution have again and again been made the basis of an argument, which regards it as a grant of political jurisdiction as well as of proprietary interest; and we humbly think it becomes him to answer that argument by something more than a begging of the question. A far greater authority than he, the greatest authority in the interpretation of the Constitution since its actual framers passed away, — Chief-Justice Marshall, — was accustomed to regard this clause as an indubitable source of political power. In a case, in the year 1810, in which he had occasion to pronounce the opinion of the Supreme Court on a question relating to the authority of Congress to confer a capacity on the citizens of a Territory to sue and be sued in a court erected by Congress for that Territory, he said, —

" The power of governing and legislating for a Territory is the inevitable consequence of the right to acquire and to hold territory. Could this position be contested, the Constitution of the United States declares that ' Congress shall have power to dispose of and make all needful rules and regulations respecting the Territory or other property belonging to the United

States.' Accordingly, we find Congress possessing and exercising the absolute and undisputed power of governing and legislating for the Territory of Orleans. Congress has given them a legislative, an executive, and a judiciary, with such powers as it has been their will to assign to those departments respectively." *

On a more recent occasion (in 1828), when Bushrod Washington, Johnson, Duval, Story, Thompson, and Trimble, were his associates, he did not hesitate, in pronouncing their opinion and his own, again to assign the same force and meaning to the Territorial clause, although he admitted that the right to govern territory might also be derived from the right to acquire it. "Whichever may be the source whence the power is derived," said the Chief-Justice, "the possession of it is unquestioned. . . . In legislating for them [the Territories], Congress exercises the combined powers of the General and of a State Government." †

While Mr. Douglas refuses to recognize that source of power which such jurists as Marshall, Washington, Story, Thompson, and their associates, regarded as amply sufficient, — namely, the Territorial clause, — he assigns the right of Congress to institute temporary governments for the Territories to the clause of the Constitution which gives power to admit new States into the Union; which, he says, taken in connection with the clause which empowers Congress "to make all laws which shall be necessary and proper" to that end, "may fairly be construed to include the right to institute temporary governments for such new States or Territories, the same as Great Britain could rightfully institute similar governments for the Colonies; but certainly not to authorize Congress to legislate in respect to their municipal affairs and internal concerns, without violating that great fundamental principle in defence of which the battles of the Revolution were fought."

We have already had occasion to suggest, that the battles of the Revolution were not fought for the purpose of ascertaining the just powers of the British Government over its Colonies, or to establish one or another doctrine of the English Constitution; but that they were fought for the expulsion of that Constitution and all its relations from

---

* Serè vs. Pitot, 6 Cranch, 332.

† American Insurance Company vs. Canter, 1 Peters, 511.

our land. Not to repeat ourselves on this point, therefore, we now proceed to consider Mr. Douglas's theory, which we understand to be this : —

That, while the right to acquire territory for the purpose of enlarging the limits of the Union by the admission of new States, and the power to admit them, necessarily involve the right to institute temporary governments, yet that the right to create a legislative department in such temporary governments, as part of the political organization, extends only to the conferring of legislative power on the people of the Territory, but does not include the power of legislating over them or for them. In support of this distinction, he refers, by way of illustration, to the right of Congress to create inferior courts, as an instance where Congress may *confer* a power which they cannot *exercise*, because Congress cannot render a judgment, or hear or determine a cause. In the same way, he says that Congress may *confer* the executive, legislative, and judicial functions on proper officers in a Territory, but that they cannot *exercise* one of those functions within the Territory.

Assuming, for the present, that the Territorial clause in the Constitution is out of the question, and that the right to acquire territory, and to form and admit new States out of it, is the source of the power to govern it, we may fairly ask, in the first place, where is the obligation to be found which imposes the necessity for creating any legislative department within the Territory when a temporary government is instituted? The power of Congress to govern, when deduced from the source above mentioned, is not less broad and general than when it is deduced from the clause giving authority to make all needful rules and regulations. In either case, there is no express limit to the power of Congress; and none is implied beyond that which the judgment of Congress may assign. The power to govern, as deduced from the power to acquire, is entirely analogous to the power which results from conquest, which is only one of the forms of acquiring; and it is as broad and universal as any political power can be. There is, therefore, no reason for saying that Congress is under any obligation to create any particular kind of temporary government for a Territory. It may be highly expedient and proper to make it a republican government, and to give to it the three regular departments of such a government, because the Territory is at some day to be admitted into the Union as a State; but we shall look into the Constitution in vain for any direction on the subject: nor can any obligation concerning the kind of government be deduced from the nature of the power, whether that power rests on one or another provision of the Constitution.

Again: if we concede the power to institute temporary governments for the Territories, as Mr. Douglas does, where can we draw the line between mere political organization and that kind of regulation which Mr. Douglas would call legislation on municipal affairs and internal concerns? What is the institution of a government, but the enactment of the fundamental law by and under which a people are to live? If a power outside of the limits of such a people is authorized to prescribe the departments of their government, the qualifications of officers and electors, and their several functions, does not the exercise of this power touch their "municipal affairs and internal concerns"? If Congress can create a legislative department in a Territorial government, can they not give or reserve just so much legislative power as they may see fit to confer or withhold? Can they not restrict the subjects of that legislative power, or make them general and universal, at pleasure? Can they not enact or adopt a code? Can they not make the reservation of a right to annul Territorial laws, or concede the legislative power without such reservation, as they may see fit? Can they not confer the legislative power on any officers to whom they may think proper to confide it? All these things have hitherto been assumed in the action of Congress to be within their legitimate functions; and, if this assumption has been wrong, the legislation of seventy years has been a series of wrongs and usurpations.

The illustration put by Mr. Douglas, of a power which may be *conferred*, but which cannot be *exercised* directly, does not afford a distinction applicable to the question. Congress cannot exercise judicial power; although it may create a court, and confer upon it judicial power. But, in the matter of instituting a government, it is legislative, not judicial power, that is exercised. The authority which can exercise the power of saying what a government is to be may make a subordinate legislature, if it sees fit; and it may confer an unrestricted or a restricted legislative faculty; and, so far as it has not parted with its original power, it may continue to exercise it. Upon any other supposition, there is no mode in which Congress can retain any control over a Territory or its inhabitants, after Congress has once erected a temporary government, or created a political organization of the people of such a Territory.

We have referred to the authority of Chief-Justice Marshall, and that of the Court over which he presided, in support of the position that the legislative power of Congress over the Territories is a plenary power, from whatever source in the Constitution it may be derived. We will next show that the Judges of the Supreme Court of the United States who are now upon the bench held the same views until the particular question respecting slavery arose in the Dred Scott case.

In 1851, the question came before the Supreme Court of the United States, whether a law enacted by a Territorial legislature, and supposed to be in conflict with a provision of the Federal Constitution, could be declared by the Supreme Court to be inoperative. The opinion of the Court was pronounced by Mr. Justice Daniel; and after pointing out the distinction between laws passed by States and laws passed by Territories, and showing that the control of the former only is vested in the Supreme Court, when they violate the Federal Constitution, he added, "It seems to us, that the control of these Territorial governments properly appertains to that branch of the government which creates and can change or modify them to meet its views of public policy; viz., the Congress of the United States." In another part of the same opinion, he shows that Territorial governments may be invested with general legislative power, and, at the same time, "be subjected to proper restraints from their superior;" viz., Congress.[*]

This decision points out very clearly the true remedy against improper or objectionable legislation by a Territorial legislature. It places the remedy in the hands of Congress, — the political "superior," as Mr. Justice Daniel appropriately calls the Federal Government, in its relation to the governments of the Territories. This idea of the "superior" power is entirely inconsistent with the "dividing line between federal and local power" which Mr. Douglas undertakes to draw. Either he is wrong, or the judges who attributed to Congress the

---

[*] Miner's Bank of Dubuque *vs.* Iowa, 12 Howard, 1.

superior and paramount authority were wrong; for it is clear that the subject of legislation of which the judges were then speaking — namely, a bank-charter — was a matter in the strictest sense belonging to the municipal affairs and internal concerns of the Territory: and, moreover, that Territory was one whose legislative power, according to the organic act, embraced "all rightful subjects of legislation;" while, at the same time, the Territorial laws were subjected by the same act to the revision of Congress.

Still more recently (in 1853), a question was before the Supreme Court, involving the validity of acts done by the Federal Government in California, after the conquest of that country, and while it was held as a Territorial possession. Mr. Justice Wayne pronounced the unanimous decision of the Bench, in which he said, —

" The Territory had been ceded as a conquest, and was to be preserved and governed as such until the sovereignty to which it had passed had legislated for it. *That sovereignty was the United States, under the Constitution, by which power had been given to Congress to dispose of and make all needful rules and regulations respecting the Territory or other property belonging to the United States, with the power also to admit new States into this Union, with only such limitations as are expressed in the section in which this power is given.* The government, of which Col. Mason was the Executive, had its origin in the lawful exercise of a belligerent right over a conquered Territory. It had been instituted during the war, by the command of the President of the United States. It was the government when the Territory was ceded as a conquest; and it did not cease as a matter of course, or as a necessary consequence of the restoration of peace. The President might have dissolved it by withdrawing the army and navy officers who administered it; but he did not do so. Congress could have put an end to it; but that was not done. The right inference from the inaction of both is, that it was meant to be continued until it had been legislatively changed. No presumption of a contrary intention can be made. Whatever may have been the causes of delay, it must be presumed that the delay was consistent with the true policy of the government; and the more so, as it was continued until the people of the Territory met in convention to form a State government; which was subsequently recognized by Congress, under its power to admit new States into the Union.

" In confirmation of what has been said in respect to the power of Congress over this Territory, and the continuance of the civil government established as a war-right until Congress acted upon the subject, we refer to two of the decisions of this Court, in one of which it is said, in respect to the treaty by which Florida was ceded to the United States, ' This treaty is the law of the land, and admits the inhabitants of Florida to the enjoyment of the privileges, rights, and immunities of the citizens of the United States. It is unnecessary to inquire whether this is not their condition, independently of stipulations. They do not, however, participate in political power: they do not share in the government until Florida shall become a State. In the mean time, Florida continues to he a Territory of the United States, governed by virtue of that clause in the Constitution which empowers Congress to make all needful rules and regulations respecting the Territory or other property belonging to the United States. Perhaps the power of governing a Territory belonging to the United States, which has not, by becoming a State, acquired the means of self-government, may result necessarily from the facts that it is not within the jurisdiction of any particular State, and is within the power and jurisdiction of the United States. The right to govern may he the natural consequence of the right to acquire territory' (American Insurance Company vs. Canter, 1 Pet. 542, 543).

"The Court afterwards, in the case of the United States vs. Gratiot, 14 Pet. 526, repeats what it said in the case of Canter, in respect to that clause of the Constitution giving to Congress the power to make all needful rules and regulations respecting the Territory or other property of the United States." *

Thus it appears, that, for a period of more than forty years, the Supreme Court has been in the habit of referring to the Territorial clause of the Constitution as an undoubted source of municipal jurisdiction; and has, in the most explicit terms, placed the sovereignty of all Territories in the government of the United States. We are therefore warranted in saying, that if any constitutional lawyer, North or South, had been asked, before the year 1856, to believe that the Territorial clause confers no municipal authority, and that "popular sovereignty" is a sound doctrine, the answer would have been, that these propositions are to be received when the Supreme Court of the United States has judicially unsaid what it has judicially said for nearly half a century.

We have thus endeavored to show, that when Mr. Douglas denies to Congress all legislative authority over the Territories, other than to institute temporary governments, he is opposed to the whole practice of Congress, and to the former and the present members of the Supreme Court of the United States; and that he is not consistent with himself, since the power to institute a government necessarily implies the authority to determine what powers that government shall possess, and

---

* Opinion of the Court in the case of Cross vs. Harrison, 16 Howard, 164.

what subjects shall be included within its legislation. We shall now refer to another of the arguments which he adduces in support of his position. We understand him to maintain, that in the word "States," in those clauses of the Constitution which require the surrender of fugitives from justice and service, and which embrace the prohibitions and restraints upon State legislation, are included the Territories as well as the States proper. Hence he argues that the people of a Territory are sovereign in the same sense in which the people of a State are sovereign, and that the sovereignty of the former is restrained and limited by the Federal Constitution in the same way in which the sovereignty of a State is restrained. This brings us to the great practical objection to Mr. Douglas's whole theory of "popular sovereignty in the Territories."

The framers of the Constitution of the United States saw occasion to subject the sovereignties of the "States" to certain restraints and prohibitions. These would all have been ineffectual and nugatory, without some means of enforcing them; and accordingly the judicial power of the United States was provided, and made to extend to "cases arising under the Constitution." In providing the machinery by which a case (arising under the Constitution because a State law is supposed to conflict with one of its provisions) may be brought within the Federal Judicial Power, the statesmen of that day framed a section of the Judiciary Act, by which such cases can be drawn into the Supreme Court of the United States, even though they originate in a State Court. But it has been repeatedly decided, that the law, whose conformity with the Federal Constitution can thus be passed upon by the Federal Judiciary, must be a law enacted by a State proper, — that is, a member of the Union; and that laws passed by Territorial legislatures are not included in this machinery of Federal judicial control. If, then, Mr. Douglas's doctrine is sound, that the word "States" in the prohibitory clauses of the Constitution includes "Territories," the first thing that strikes us is, that there are no means provided by which the Federal Government can enforce these provisions of the Constitution against the legislation of Territories, unless Congress reserves to itself a power directly to annul the Territorial laws. Such a reservation is plainly inconsistent with Mr. Douglas's theory; for he insists that Congress has no power to control the people of a Territory in respect to their domestic concerns. But as he qualifies this position with the reservation, that their domestic legislation must not violate the provisions of the Federal Constitution, he may still retain to Congress so much superintending power as is necessary to preserve the Federal Constitution intact. But the difficulty in the way of his theory is, that if the Constitution, when it says the "States" shall not do certain things, also means the "Territories," we have got two classes of sovereignties in our system, both of which are subjected to the same restraints by the Federal Constitution; but those restraints are to be enforced, as against the States, by the Judicial, and as against the Territories by the Legislative, department of the Federal Government.

This discrepancy naturally leads to the inquiry, what reason there is for supposing that when the framers of the Constitution provided that no "State" shall pass laws impairing the obligation of contracts, or emit bills of credit, &c., they intended to be understood as extending these same prohibitions to "Territories," which could only owe their existence to Acts of Congress. It is notorious, that all these prohibitions were inserted in the Constitution to prevent the repetition of acts of wrong that had previously been committed by the legislatures of sovereign States, members of the Union; or to secure the just working of the powers conferred on the National Government. But if we suppose that the framers of the Constitution intended to have Congress invested with power to erect temporary governments in regions beyond the limits of the then existing States, as Mr. Douglas concedes they did, there is no conceivable reason why they should not have left to Congress to put upon those governments just such restraints as the occasion might require; nor why they should have included those governments in the prohibitions addressed to the "States;" nor why they should have used the word "States" alone, if they meant "States" and "Territories." The view that was taken by Mr. Justice Daniel explains the true reason why Congress should be regarded as the "superior" of the Territories; for there may be a vast deal of legislation by a Territory, which would violate no provision of the Federal Constitution, but would yet be exceedingly objectionable, and ought to be corrected, and could be if Congress has the superior authority attributed to it by the Supreme Court in the case to which we have referred. But if Congress is the political "superior" only so far as to see that the Federal Constitution is not infringed, then indeed the Territorial legislature, which is the mere creature of Congress, may make lawful a plurality of wives, or establish the most pernicious system of banking, or create a most objectionable system of divorce, — may make the Territory a nuisance and a pest to the surrounding communities; and there will be no earthly power that can interfere, whether Congress has or has not reserved the right to revise the Territorial laws. For if Mr. Douglas's doctrine is correct, that, in all domestic affairs, the people of the Territory are sovereign just as the people of a State are sovereign, all such reservations are simply void.

We protest, therefore, against this popular cry, which seeks to class the pretended sovereignties of the Territories with the sovereignties of the States. We are neither anxious nor alarmed about the matter of slavery. We are not disposed to look at every doctrine solely as it affects this particular institution. We seek no sectional triumphs on this or any other subject. In a particular case of real fitness for a fair and unbiased decision as to their true interests, we should have no unwillingness to see the people of a Territory invested, by Act of Congress, with full power to decide whether they would have slavery or not; although we never could see its propriety in the case of Kansas, and think that the whole country has infinite cause to regret, that, in this case, a new and unoccupied region was made a battle-field for the contending sections of the Union. But, however this may be, we protest against an effort, by means of a clamor about popular sovereignty, which tends to wrench the Constitution out of its appropriate sphere, to render its harmonious action impracticable, and to throw unlimited political authority into the hands of communities which may require, for their own good and the good of the country, the strong restraining hand of a "superior." Train the people of every Territory, as fast as you practicably can, in the business of self-government; but do not begin with ignoring your duty to deal out political power just as fast as they can safely be intrusted with it, and no faster, merely because you desire to contrive a short-hand method of disposing of the "slavery question," or to avoid the responsibilities which that question involves. If you believe that the Constitution, *proprio vigore*, carries slavery into the Territories, march up to the point, and say so. If you believe that it does not, but that legislation is necessary to plant slavery there, vote *yes* or *no* when such legislation is proposed. If you think it inexpedient to have the question decided while the Territorial condition continues, place that question in abeyance by suitable provisions. If you wish to leave it to the people of a particular Territory to decide it for themselves before they acquire the right of self-government by becoming a sovereign State, confer on them the necessary power. But take care how you emasculate the Constitution by a doctrine which will return to plague your invention in a hundred ways, and will render the full and free administration of the Federal Government impracticable, by making the sovereignties of the States and the sovereignties of the Territories one and the same.

The sovereignties of the "States" are founded in something more than an *abstract right* of self-government. We are not to forget that they are older than the Federal Constitution; that the Federal system itself is the embodiment of certain portions of sovereign power which the States originally held, but which they found it convenient and necessary to part with, and to vest in a central authority, for their common good; and that if, for the same great object of the common good, they deemed it necessary to convey to that central authority their several claims to unoccupied territory, or their several rights to acquire territory outside of their respective limits, it is not a very probable supposition that they intended to convey their political jurisdiction over such regions to any power but that which they had instituted as their common agent for the accomplishment of the objects which they had in view. They held, without doubt, most tenaciously to their right of popular sovereignty; that is, the right of self-government. But this right, as embodied in the idea of State sovereignty, is founded, likewise, in the proud consciousness of capacity for its exercise. That lofty State independence, which feels an encroachment like a wound, is the result of conscious fitness for the condition which it jealously guards, and which use has made normal. How strange it seems, that political societies, which have thus blended together in their own existence the ideas of an abstract right and a capacity of self-government, should be supposed to lay the former only at the foundation of new communities, and to treat the latter as of no account in the formation of a system for the creation of new members of their general confederacy! Again and again has each generation, since the Federal Constitution was established, witnessed the settlement of Territories, whose inhabitants, in the earlier stages of their career, have been practically incapable of holding and fulfilling the trusts of a full self-government. How can it be otherwise in sparsely settled regions, where the people have not been accustomed to act together; where they come from communities of differing political ideas; where some have had no civil training at all, where others are entirely lawless, while a few are perhaps skilled in all the arts of political management; where no homogeneous popular character has been formed; and where there are as yet none of the institutions which brace society together, and none of the settled habits of order which precedents supply? When we consider what legislation sometimes results from general suffrage, even in our oldest States, we cannot see in the doctrine of popular sovereignty in the Territories, with all that is claimed for it by one of the wings of modern democracy, any thing that should cause us to embrace it for its wisdom and expediency, any more than for its conformity to sound constitutional principle.

We have said that the sovereignties of the States are founded in something more than an abstract or natural right. Let us now add to the illustrations which we have already suggested upon this point the further fact, that the very idea of State sovereignty involves the existence of some system of fundamental law, which we call a constitution. No one can conceive of a State, a sovereign member of this Union, without some restraints of fundamental law, — self-imposed, it is true, and resting upon the popular will, but defining the limits of legislative power, operating to protect the minority against the majority, the weak against the strong, and preventing the government from being the mere despotism of an irresponsible mob. It is the presence of these restraints on popular power — voluntarily assumed, but at the same time solemnly incorporated into public compacts — which makes a democracy a republic, and secures the individual against injustice and oppression. Without this high achievement in political science, the sovereignty of a State would be destitute of its noblest attribute. This is the diadem which popular sovereignty places upon its own brow; and, if it were lost, all would indeed be lost with it.

But how can these restraints, or any fundamental law whatever, save the act of Congress which organizes it, exist in a Territory?

There, no local constitution throws its shield over private or public rights. There, if we accept the theory of "popular sovereignty" which we are invited to embrace, there can be no restraints upon the absolute will of the majority; and legislation may be, as we have seen it in Kansas, violent, proscriptive, and tyrannical, disgraceful to the age, and shocking to the common sense of mankind, without the least remedy on earth for the individual, because there is no test of established principle, in the nature of a Bill of Rights, to which such legislation can be brought. In a Territory, there is absolutely nothing that can answer to the place of a Bill of Rights for individuals; and there is nothing that can fill this place, for the Territories, except the large superintending discretion of Congress, — the public conscience of the nation, — which can watch the Territorial legislation, and can restrain it where it ought to be restrained.

If we look to the practical benefits which are expected from this new doctrine of "popular sovereignty," in reference to "the slavery question," we see still less to hope from it. The grand recommendation with which it is presented to us is, that it will prevent agitation of the slavery question in Congress. In the session of 1853–4, Mr. Douglas carried his point. He procured the repeal of the Missouri Compromise, and obtained a Congressional declaration, that the Federal authority would neither put slavery into or put it out of Kansas, but that the people of that Territory should be perfectly free to decide this question for themselves. We were told that this legislation was to put the slavery question and all agitation of it out of Congress, and that universal peace was to reign. We may give all credit to Mr. Douglas for patriotic motives; but how has his experiment succeeded? For five years, we believe, there has not been a session of Congress during which this subject has not been discussed. It could not have been otherwise. The direct consequence of throwing this matter into Kansas, to be acted upon there in the legislative body, in the attempts to make constitutions, in the struggles of parties, reenforced as they were by outside intermeddlers, was, that an almost countless series of questions was thrown back into Congress, invoking and precipitating constant agitation of the subject of slavery. "Topeca" and "Lecompton," of necessity, claimed the intervention which the organic act had vainly undertaken to forestall and prevent.

It is not extravagant to say, that there has been more and worse agitation of "the slavery question" in Congress, in the last five years, in consequence of this effort to put the subject out of Congress, than could have taken place if the National Legislature had proceeded, after having made a clean field by removing the Missouri restriction, to consider anew, on grounds of expediency, whether slavery should or should not be directly introduced and legalized in that unhappy Territory.

If we turn to the state of things that has existed in Kansas itself, we cannot fail to see the utter futility of the hope that the Federal Government would be relieved from embarrassment by remitting the decision respecting slavery to the supreme arbitrament of "popular sovereignty." The Federal Executive was forced to remove governor after governor, and secretary after secretary, because "the policy of the administration," in respect to the principles of the organic act and its requirements, was supposed to be misunderstood or misinterpreted by those local functionaries. The Territory was torn by factions, whose struggles created a civil confusion amounting nearly or quite to civil war, in which the intervention of the National Government became absolutely unavoidable. This intervention carried with it, naturally, inevitably, some further display of "the policy of the administration." That policy was supposed, rightfully or wrongfully, to have a leaning on the subject of slavery. The acts of the Executive and its supposed policy could not escape examination in Congress; and the whole circumstances of the case led to discussions, which opened again and again the widest door for the introduction of bitter sectional controversy.

As it has been, so it will be again if a similar course is again pursued. The expedient of "popular sovereignty" will be of no more efficacy in keeping the subject of slavery out of Congress hereafter than it has been heretofore. If all branches of the Government and a majority of the people of the whole country were to acquiesce in the doctrine that Congress cannot rightfully legislate directly on the subject of slavery in the Territories, it would still be in the power of Congress to exert an indirect influence; that influence would be invoked; and the invoking of it would produce agitation, as extensive, as fierce, and as dangerous as any discussion of a proslavery or an antislavery bill. For if we suppose the case of a Territory whose inhabitants, proceeding to decide this question for themselves, had evidently determined to decide it against the wishes of a majority, or even of a strong minority, of the States, as represented in Congress, it would be impossible for them to deal with it in such a way as to remove it out of the indirect reach of that majority or minority. The opportunities for throwing impediments in their way, without direct violation of their "sovereignty," would be endless; and those opportunities would produce Congressional agitation. Kansas, with all the boasted non-intervention of its organic act, has proved this to demonstration.

Another of the practical benefits which Mr. Douglas seems to promise himself will flow from the doctrine of "popular sovereignty" is that it will furnish an answer to the extreme Southern pretension, that slavery goes into a Territory by force of the Constitution of the United States, and that the people of the Territory cannot legislate to keep it out. He denies that this pretension has received any sanction from the opinions expressed by the majority of the Judges in the Dred Scott case; and he maintains, that, while those opinions sustain his denial of the power of Congress to legislate directly against the introduction of slavery into a Territory, they do not negative the power of the people of the Territory to exclude it by their own action. We differ entirely from Mr. Douglas in respect to this point; and will now proceed to show why the views expressed in the case of Dred Scott are entirely irreconcilable with his doctrine of "popular sovereignty."

It is difficult to speak of the case of Dred Scott with proper precision. To call it a *decision*, without a great deal of discrimination, is quite incorrect. The *conclusion* arrived at by a majority of the Court was, that the plaintiff could not maintain his action. But most lawyers, who have examined the case critically, are aware, that in consequence of the peculiar state of the record, as it came before the Supreme Court, the views expressed by the several Judges (who united in the above-mentioned *conclusion*), respecting the legislative power of Congress over the Territories, do not constitute a *judicial decision*, so as to overrule the series of former cases, which had affirmed that Congress possesses a municipal authority over the Territories by virtue of what has been called the Territorial clause of the Constitution * (Art. iv.

---

* See the note on the Dred Scott case, in the APPENDIX, A.

4

sect. 3). At the same time, it is undoubtedly true, that a majority of the Judges did give their personal sanction to two propositions: *first*, that Congress derives no municipal authority over the Territories from the Territorial clause; and, *secondly*, that, whatever its authority may be, slave *property* cannot be excluded by *Congress* from any place where Congress has jurisdiction. Now, in order to see whether the same Judges did not equally maintain that the Territorial legislature is also destitute of power to exclude slave *property*, we have only to look at the opinion of the Chief-Justice, which was written and read as the opinion of a majority of the Court. From that opinion, we maintain that Mr. Douglas can derive no support for the power of a Territorial legislature to exclude slavery; but that, on the contrary, the opinion negatives the power of both Territory and Congress.

The Chief-Justice maintains, that while Congress may have an implied power to regulate the political organization of a Territory, in order to prepare it for admission as a State, yet that Congress has no power of legislation which can reach a subject to which the Constitution has extended its protection, which it has placed under certain guaranties, and which is, therefore, as fully excluded from the control of Congress as if it were named in an express prohibition. In order to establish the last of these conclusions, the venerable Chief-Justice refers to the express prohibitions which the Constitution has imposed as restrictions upon the powers of Congress, — such as the prohibition against making laws respecting an establishment of religion; the quartering of soldiers in time of peace; the depriving any person of life, liberty, or property, without due process of law, &c., — and he shows conclusively, that neither in a Territory nor in a State can Congress exercise any power over the person or property of a citizen, beyond what the Constitution confers, or lawfully deny any right which it has reserved. This position, which is taken with great strength, and which no Constitutional lawyer will contest, is thus summed up by the Chief-Justice: —

"The powers over person and property of which we speak are not only not granted to Congress, but are in express terms denied; and they are [it is] forbidden to exercise them. And the prohibition is not confined to the States; but the words are general, and extend to the whole Territory over which the Constitution gives it [Congress] power to legislate, including those portions of it remaining under Territorial government, as well as that covered by States. It is a total absence of power everywhere within the dominion of the United States, and places the citizens of a Territory, so far as these rights are concerned, on the same footing with citizens of the States, and guards them as firmly and plainly against any inroads which the General Government might attempt under the plea of implied or incidental powers. And, if Congress itself cannot do this, — if it is beyond the powers conferred on the Federal Government, — it will be admitted, we presume, that it could not authorize a Territorial government to exercise them. It could confer no power on any local government, established by its authority, to violate the provisions of the Constitution." *

From this, it is sufficiently apparent that the Chief-Justice meant to lay it down as a proposition which admitted of no denial or exception, that where there is a right secured or guaranteed by the Constitution, or a prohibition imposed on the legislative power of Congress which that body is forbidden to violate by its own action, the Territorial legislature is equally forbidden; because Congress cannot authorize any body to do that which it is itself prohibited from doing. Now, the mode in which the Chief-Justice places slavery within this undeniable principle is this, — that although the Constitution contains no express prohibition against the passing of laws respecting slavery, yet that it manifestly withholds the power to decide what is or is not to be regarded as property; that it not only withholds this power, but that it recognizes the right of property of the master in a slave, and recognizes no distinction between that and all other property; that, this right of the master being thus recognized by the Constitution as a right of property, no tribunal, acting under the authority of the United States, can take away that property without due process of law; and that a legislative act forbidding a citizen to bring his property into a particular Territory would deprive him of it " without due process of law." — " And if the Constitution," says the Chief-Justice, " recognizes the right of property of the master in a slave, and makes no distinction between that description of property and other property owned by a citizen, no tribunal acting under the authority of the United States — whether it be legislative, executive, or judicial — has a right to draw such a distinction, or deny to it the benefit of the provisions and guaranties

---

* Opinion of Mr. Chief-Justice Taney in the case of Dred Scott, 19 Howard, 450.

which have been provided for the protection of private property against the encroachments of the government."

Hence it is quite plain, that when Mr. Douglas reads the opinion of the Chief-Justice as if, in speaking of those things which neither Congress nor its creature the Territory can do, he intended to embrace only the express prohibitions of the Constitution, and *therefore* did not mean to exclude " the slavery question " from the legislative power of a Territory, he does not appreciate the Chief-Justice's argument: for it is clear, from the whole tenor of that argument, that it meant to bring slave property, as property, within the protection of the Constitution, and to deny that there is any authority in any legislative body, organized under the Constitution, to exclude it from any place where such body has jurisdiction ; because such exclusion would be a depriving the citizen of his property " without due process of law ; " which cannot be done, either by the Territory or by Congress.

We are not at present concerned with what we believe to be the true answer to this argument ; but we wish to impress upon our readers, that every thing depends upon the truth and extent of the two postulates, — *first,* that the Constitution recognizes, and means to protect, slaves as property ; and, *secondly,* that to legislate for its exclusion from a particular place, which is under the jurisdiction of Congress, violates that provision of the Constitution which declares that " no person shall be deprived of life, liberty, or property, without due process of law."

If these positions are well taken, the conclusion is inevitable, that neither Congress nor the Territorial legislature can prevent the introduction of such property into any Territory of the United States.

We may well ask, then, of what avail is " popular sovereignty " to be against this doctrine ? Mr. Douglas himself allows, that the sovereignty of the people of a Territory is subject to the restraints imposed by the Constitution of the United States. Indeed, it would be impossible for him to construct his theory upon any other basis ; for whether the sovereignties of the Territories are or are not to be regarded as subjected to the same restraints which are imposed upon the sovereignties of the States, it is certain that the legislative power of a Territory, which is called into existence by the action of Congress, can have no greater latitude than the Constitution allows to the power of Congress itself. "Popular sovereignty," therefore, can furnish no answer to the doctrine which a majority of the Judges of the Supreme Court unquestionably did sanction in the case of Dred Scott, although the technical posture of the record in that case was not such as to give their affirmance of this doctrine the force of a judicial precedent. That doctrine can only be met by asserting the general legislative authority of Congress over the Territories, and by showing that this authority is not restrained in respect to slavery in the mode contended for by the Chief-Justice.

This last position is to be established by showing that the Constitution simply recognizes the fact, that in certain of the States there are persons who, by the local laws of those States, owe service to certain other persons ; that this relation, founded in the local law, is recognized beyond the dominion of that law, only in the exceptional case of an escape into a State to whose local law it is unknown ; and that, as it is competent to a State to make the law of personal relations within its own limits (subject to the exception of an escape), it is in the same way competent to Congress to make that law where Congress has exclusive jurisdiction ; namely, in the Territories.*

No one can have observed attentively the signs of the times, without perceiving the influence which the doctrine of "popular sovereignty" has had, and is yet likely to have, in promoting the extreme Southern claim for an active interference by Congress to protect slave property in the Territories. In this respect, we look upon this doctrine as one of the worst among the various provocatives of sectional agitation. There are many politicians, and other persons who are not politicians, in the South, who feel strongly on the subject of their general claim to emigrate into regions which confessedly belong to the people of the whole Union, and to carry with them that form of labor to which they are accustomed. They know that Congress is the administrator of the public domains of the Union, in trust for the common good ; and, in a pending case, they would feel the necessity, and at the same time the equity, of an appeal to Congress to give them that protection without

* See the note on the property doctrine, in the APPENDIX, B.

which their abstract claim of right would be of no value. But the doctrine of "popular sovereignty" turns them away from the doors of Congress, — the legitimate umpire with respect to their claim to share in the common domain, — and sends them to a tribunal where they may not be represented, and where, if they are represented, the decision may be nothing but the result of a social scramble. Who can wonder, then, that they are driven by this new dogma into the maintenance of a theory that will override it? — the theory that the Constitution itself protects slaves as property, and that, where the jurisdiction of Congress exists, it is bound to legislate for the protection of that which the Constitution sanctions and recognizes. You propose to deny them a hearing in Congress, and to send them before the people of a Territory for a decision of a purely equitable claim, which addresses itself to the national justice. If you thus ignore your duty to decide, how can you expect that they will not convert their equitable claim into a claim of positive right, and thus circumvent you if they can?

We have no faith in any of the expedients for quieting sectional controversy which involve a negation of the proper duty of Congress. All such expedients have a necessary tendency to multiply the occasions and causes of strife. If either section of the Union were to be outvoted in Congress on the direct question of slavery in a Territory, the mischiefs to be apprehended from the result would bear no comparison with such a state of things as that which followed the reference of this question to the people of Kansas.

Having thus endeavored to show that "popular sovereignty" is likely to be attended with no practical advantages, we beg leave to ask of our Democratic friends, why they cannot cease to agitate about the means of putting an end to agitation. If any voice of ours could reach them, we would respectfully but firmly inquire of the great Democratic party of this country, what they expect to gain by the establishment of this theory of popular sovereignty in the Territories, if they shall adopt it, and shall succeed in carrying a popular election by it, as the means of disposing of "the slavery question." Whether rightfully or wrongfully maintained, when a Presidential election is carried upon a Constitutional doctrine, that doctrine becomes, in the practical administration of the government, a settled construction, — at least, for the party which adopts it, — however ill adapted the popular tribunal may be for the correct decision of such a question. The Democratic party, therefore, if it succeeds upon this doctrine, will consistently adhere to it. It will administer the government, in respect to the affairs of all Territories, upon the principle laid down by Mr. Douglas; namely, that Congress has no power to interfere in respect to their local or municipal affairs. It will organize all Territories, hereafter, not simply with a concession of " popular sovereignty " on this particular matter of slavery, but without any reservation to Congress of the least control over the Territorial legislation on any domestic subject whatever. Let the mischiefs of that legislation be what they may, the Democratic party must reap as it shall have sown, and can only profess the inability of the Federal power to afford either preventive or cure.

Are our Democratic countrymen prepared for this surrender of the authority of Congress? If they would fall back, in respect to the mere " slavery question," upon the doctrine of a majority of the Judges in the Dred Scott case, and would say that the legislative authority of Congress is restrained, because the *property* character of slavery brings it within one of the positive prohibitions which the Constitution has laid upon all the powers of Congress, their course would be intelligible, unsound as we might be disposed to regard it. But they are urged to go much beyond this: they are counselled to abrogate the entire legislative and superintending jurisdiction of Congress over the Territories, without looking to see whether a case of special prohibition is or is not made out. For ourselves, we do not mean to consent to this abdication in favor of the people of any Territory, on the slavery or any other question, however willing we might be to *confer* on them the faculty of self-government in suitable cases.

To show that we have not overstated the consequences of a general denial of the municipal authority of Congress over the Territories, we desire to vouch the testimony of Mr. Justice Catron, — a man of great fearlessness, a citizen of a slaveholding State, and, in his early days, a political disciple of Andrew Jackson; whose life and actions certainly tended to any thing rather than to a diminution of the Federal powers.

In considering the various grounds on which the Court had been urged, in the Dred Scott case, to decide that Congress could not legislate to exclude slavery from a Territory, Judge Catron was evidently struck with the consequences of that sweeping denial of the general authority of Congress over Territories, which is embraced in the political phrase "popular sovereignty." He knew, that, in regions beyond the Mississippi, his official duty had, for nearly twenty years, called upon him to perform judicial acts whose validity rested on the lawful supremacy of Congress over the Territories and their inhabitants; and that, sitting on the Supreme Bench at Washington, he had united with his brethren in declaring that that supremacy rests upon the power "to make all needful rules and regulations" for such Territories. When, therefore, he came to announce his concurrence with those of his brethren who held the Missouri-Compromise restriction void, he used the following significant language; which we commend to all advocates of the doctrine of "popular sovereignty," as it is expounded by Mr. Douglas : —

"It was hardly possible [in framing the Constitution] to separate the power ' to make all needful rules and regulations ' respecting the government of the Territory, and the disposition of the public lands. . . . It is due to myself to say, that it is asking much of a Judge who has, for nearly twenty years, been exercising jurisdiction from the western Missouri line to the Rocky Mountains, and, on this understanding of the Constitution, inflicting the extreme penalty of death for crimes committed where the direct legislation of Congress was the only rule, to agree that he had been, all the while, acting in mistake and as an usurper.

"More than sixty years have passed away since Congress has exercised power to govern the Territories by its legislation directly, or by Territorial charters subject to repeal at all times; and it is now too late to call that power into question, if this Court could disregard its own decisions; which it cannot do, as I think. It was held, in the case of Cross *vs.* Harrison (16 Howard, 193–4), that the sovereignty of California was in the United States in virtue of the Constitution, by which power had been given to Congress to dispose of, and make all needful rules and regulations respecting, the territory or other property belonging to the United States, with the power to admit new States into the Union. That decision followed preceding ones there cited. The question was then presented, how it was possible for the judicial mind to conceive that the United-States Government, created solely by the Constitution, could, by a lawful treaty, acquire territory over which the acquiring power had no jurisdiction to hold and govern it, by force of the instrument under whose authority the country was acquired; and the foregoing was the conclusion of this Court on the proposition. What was there announced was most deliberately done, and with a purpose. *The only question here is, as I think, how far the power of Congress is limited."* [*]

In conclusion, we have only to say, that it has for some years excited our special wonder to observe how politicians and parties, and even the people of the United States, go on in reference to this relation of the Federal Government to the Territories, apparently without thinking of that portentous cloud which hangs upon our Western horizon, — the Territory of Utah. The country is actually about to be precipitated into a Presidential election, in which the sweeping doctrine is to be proclaimed, — perhaps to be sanctioned, — that the Federal power can exercise no interference whatever with the local and municipal concerns of the inhabitants of any of its Territories; while, at this very day, a problem is before us at which statesmen may stand aghast, and which may call for all the Constitutional power that our fathers devised, and for all the physical resources that the country can spare, to enforce its supremacy.

With respect to the topic of slavery, as involved in the exercise of the jurisdiction which we contend rightfully belongs to Congress in all the Territories, we desire to say, that we advocate and earnestly pray for a return, if such a return be possible, to the policy of those who founded the Federal Government, and who administered it with the knowledge which, as its founders, they must have possessed. That policy was as far removed from all previous or abstract popular agitation of this question as it was eminently liberal, wise, and practical. Our fathers waited until they had a Territory to organize and a Territorial government to provide. When this practical duty was before them, they inquired who were the present, or who were likely to be the future, settlers; what would subserve the interests, or be in accordance with the wishes, of those settlers; and, if the circumstances by which the case was surrounded seemed to require it, they sought for such a compromise of the merely sectional demands involved in it as justice, fairness, and comity would dictate. In this way, while they endeavored to guard the Southern

---

[*] Opinion of Mr. Justice Catron in the case of Dred Scott, 19 Howard, 522–3.

Territories (even before the year 1808) against the introduction of fresh slaves from Africa, they permitted Southern men to enter those Territories with the slaves which they already possessed. In this way, too, they succeeded, both before and after the Constitution, in impressing an unalterable condition of freedom upon the whole region northwest of the Ohio. They thus made Free States and Slave States, side by side, without sectional feuds, down to the time of the Missouri Compromise, which was the first occasion on which this question seriously threatened the harmony of the Union. How the dangers of that occasion were avoided, all of us understand.

Since that period, what has the history of the country demonstrated? It has shown, beyond the possibility of denial, that, whenever popular agitation begins in reference to what is called the *extension* of slavery, it inevitably runs into a chronic inflammation of the sectional passions, engendering extravagant doctrines and unreasonable demands, at both ends of the Union. In the South, such doctrines and demands take the shape of a revival of the slave-trade, and the scriptural warrant for slavery : in the North, a fierce and uncalled-for hostility to the special feature of Southern society becomes developed into plots and conspiracies for the liberation of those over whose condition we have neither a legal nor a moral right of jurisdiction, and in the execution of which not a single step can be taken without bloodshed. Now, unless we mean to go on in this way until we have created both a civil and a servile war for the gratification of a few madmen, we must consider what are our duties, and must proceed resolutely to discharge them.

One of the first of our duties, which is as much incumbent on the people of the South as it is on the people of the North, is to divest ourselves of the influence which an exaggerated sense of the importance of this Territorial-*slavery* question has exerted over our minds. It has been found, in both sections, to be an engine useful to the politician. This very capacity of the subject — its capacity to win votes for parties or individuals — should lead us to watch its treatment with the utmost jealousy, and to watch its influence over ourselves. If, in so doing, the people of either section would calmly consider what degree of practical importance belongs at any time to this question, apart from all other matters involved in the relation of the Federal Government to the

Territories, they would find that its chief value consists in its power of creating political excitement; or, in other words, in its power for mischief. This being the case, our next imperative duty is to make ourselves fully sensible of the fact, that neither of the political parties, which are responsible for the agitation of this question, has dealt with it wisely or properly. The Democratic party, for example, found this question, six years ago, in reference to all the territory then demanding organization, settled by a compromise which had stood on the statute-book for more than thirty years. They repealed that settlement; from what motive, we do not now inquire. They thus repudiated the policy of settling the character of particular Territories by Congressional compromise or arrangement; and, *so far as they could do it, rendered a resort to that ancient and peaceful method exceedingly difficult, if not impracticable, hereafter.* They thus entailed upon themselves the necessity of finding some rule, of a universal and permanent character, which would furnish a solution of the difficulty created by their abrogation of the old policy. In pursuit of this rule, they have been ever since —

" In wandering mazes lost."

Agreeing only in their repudiation of the power of *Congress* to *prohibit* slavery in a Territory, they present the spectacle of a great national party seeking in the most contradictory ways for an answer to the question, — which they never should have suffered to arise, — *What is the true condition of a Territory, when there is neither prohibition nor sanction of slavery by Congressional interference?*

We say this in no spirit of triumph or exultation; for we regard it as a national misfortune, when a political party, strong by its ramifications throughout the country, and renowned for its fidelity to the Union, paralyzes its own power of usefulness by such a course. It is difficult to conceive of a greater political error than the one that was thus committed by the Democratic party. It immediately gave rise to what ought to have been foreseen, — the pretension, on the part of their extreme Southern wing, that slavery goes into a Territory against the will of both Congress and the people of that Territory; while it compelled the Northern portion of the same party to look about for a doctrine on which they can exist in the Free States, and to find it in " popular sovereignty," which overturns the supremacy of Congress on a vast many other subjects as well as on the subject of slavery.*

But this was not all, if it was even half, of the evil. A political party must have an antagonist in every free, constitutional government; and, although the Democracy succeeded in scattering their ancient opponents, another organization arose to be their adversaries. The denial by the Democratic party of the power of Congress to exclude slavery from a Territory, led the Republicans, of course, to embrace and defend that power; and, if the Republicans had contented themselves with the discharge of this obvious duty, they might have restored the Constitution to its true position, and have earned for themselves a title to be called benefactors of their country. This was their mission; and rarely has there been a higher one presented to any political organization. But, easy as it may be to trace their error, it is not so easy to excuse it. They should have made themselves the defenders of the supremacy of Congress over the Territories, and should have vindicated its *power* to deal with slavery therein, as with all other things, whether by compromise, or by naked legislation without compromise. But here they should have stopped.

Instead of this, they mingled with this great argument — which demanded Southern as well as Northern support, and to which the South should have been won by the power of reason and the persuasive gentleness of brotherly love — the untenable dogma, offensive at once to Southern pride, that the power is a power to prohibit, and includes no authority to establish or sanction, slavery. They declared, that, every-

---

* As we write these paragraphs, we read in the "Chicago Times," a paper in the interest of Mr. Douglas, that, "from the day of Mr. Douglas's triumph in Congress over the administration in the affair of Lecompton, he has been denounced as a traitor, and every man has been proscribed who avowed sympathy or conviction with him. The masterly Essay on 'The Dividing Line between Local and Federal Authority' thus became necessary, as well to his own vindication *as for the rescue of the party from impending ruin.*"

An impartial spectator cannot fail to ask why it is that the Democratic party is exposed to "impending ruin;" and such a spectator cannot avoid seeing, that when a political party departs from established principles of the Constitution, seeking for new theories to take the place of plain Constitutional powers long recognized and acted upon, it must necessarily become divided against itself in the pursuit of such theories. Had the Missouri Compromise been left undisturbed, neither Mr. Douglas nor "the administration" would ever have had occasion to contend about "popular sovereignty in the Territories."

where and under all circumstances, the slaveholder shall be excluded
from the national domains, if he goes with the servants whom he
possesses at home. They sought to rouse the Free States, by a general
antislavery agitation, to a combination for the enforcement of a policy,
the declaration of which increased instead of diminishing the perils to
which the Constitutional power was already exposed. These were acts
of consummate imprudence. They were acts which gave the control of
the Republican party to its least reliable members; made its fanatics
leaders; and, of necessity, reduced it to the position of a purely sectional
organization, to be feared and abhorred throughout one-half of the
Union. Over this error, too, we have no feeling of gratification to
indulge. It is mournful to see a noble cause frustrated by those to whose
hands fortune has committed its defence. It is mournful to see a great
Constitutional power which was lodged by our fathers in their frame of
government, for wise and beneficent purposes, and which can alone
furnish a safe means of disposing of questions which imperil our peace,
thus put still further from its office by the indiscretion of those who
ought to have gained for it the glad acquiescence of the whole land, by
making the South to feel that her interest in its maintenance is even
greater than the interest of the North.

APPENDIX.

A.

Note on the Dred Scott Case, referred to ante, p. 25.

THE decision of the Supreme Court of the United States in the Dred Scott case is so little understood, and its character as a judicial precedent is so generally misapprehended and so often misrepresented, that the following analysis of it may be useful.

The plaintiff, Dred Scott, brought an action of trespass in the Circuit Court of the United States for the District of Missouri, against the defendant, Sandford, for the purpose of establishing his freedom; and according to the requirements of law, in order to gain the jurisdiction of the Court, the plaintiff, in his writ, averred himself to be a "citizen" of the State of Missouri, and the defendant to be a "citizen" of the State of New York. The defendant filed a plea in abatement, alleging that the plaintiff is not a "citizen" of Missouri, because he is a negro of African descent, his ancestors having been of pure African blood, brought into this country and sold as slaves. To this plea the plaintiff demurred; and, as by his demurrer he admitted the *facts* alleged in the plea, the sole question on the demurrer was the question of law, whether a negro of African descent, whose *ancestors* were slaves, can be a citizen of the United States, for the purpose of suing a citizen of another State than his own in a Circuit Court. The Circuit Court gave judgment for the plaintiff on this question; and the defendant was ordered to plead to the merits of the action. He did so; and the substance of his plea in bar of the action was, that the plaintiff was his (the defendant's) slave, and that he had a right to restrain him as such. Upon the issue joined upon this allegation, the case went to trial upon the merits, under an agreed statement of facts, which ascertained, in substance, that the plaintiff, who was a slave in Missouri in 1834, was carried by his then master into the State of Illinois, and afterwards into that part of the Louisiana Territory in which slavery had been prohibited by the act of Congress called the Missouri Compromise, and was afterwards brought back to Missouri, and held and sold as a slave. The jury, under the instructions of the Court, found that the plaintiff, at the time of bringing his action, was a slave; and the defendant obtained judgment. The plaintiff then sued out a writ of error to the Supreme Court of the United States, which removed the whole record into that Court.

It will be observed that the record, as brought into the Supreme Court, presented two questions : —

1. The question arising on the plea to the jurisdiction of the Circuit Court, whether a negro of African descent, whose *ancestors* were *slaves*, can be a *citizen.*

2. The question involved in the verdict and judgment on the merits, whether the *plaintiff* was a *slave* at the time he brought his action. This question involved, among others, the inquiry whether the Missouri Compromise, which prohibited the existence of slavery in the Territory where the plaintiff was carried, was constitutional or not.

The importance and effect of the *Dred Scott decision* depend entirely upon the manner in which these questions were dealt with by the Supreme Court. If either of them was *judicially* decided by a majority of the Bench in the same way, the decision constitutes a judicial precedent, binding upon the Court hereafter, and upon all other persons and tribunals, until it is reversed in the same Court, to just the extent that such decision goes. If either of them was not judicially decided by a majority of the Bench in the same way, there is no precedent and no decision on the subject ; and the case embraces only certain individual opinions of the judges. The following analysis will determine what has been judicially decided. The reader will observe, that, when the *plea in abatement* is spoken of, it means that part of the pleadings which raised the question whether a negro can be a citizen : the *merits of the action* comprehend the question whether the plaintiff was a *slave,* as affected by the operation of the Missouri Compromise, or otherwise. Keeping these points in view, every reader of the case should endeavor to ascertain the true answers to the following questions : —

I. How many of the judges, and which of them, held that the plea in abatement was rightfully before the Court, on the writ of error, so that they must pass upon the question whether a negro can be a citizen ?

Answer. — Four : Chief-Justice, and Justices Wayne, Daniel, and Curtis.

II. Of the above four, how many expressed the opinion that a negro can *not* be a citizen ?

Answer. — Three : Chief-Justice, and Justices Wayne and Daniel.

Judge Curtis, who agreed that the plea in abatement was rightfully before the Court, held that a negro *may* be a citizen, and that the Circuit Court, therefore, rightfully had jurisdiction of the case.

The opinions of these four judges on this question are to be regarded as *judicial*; they having held that the record authorized and required its decision. But as there are only three of them on one side of the question, and there is one on the other, and there were five other judges on the bench, there is no judicial majority upon this question, unless two at least of the other five concurred in the opinion that the question arising on the plea in abatement was to be decided by the Supreme Court, and *also* took the same view of that question with Judges Taney, Wayne, and Daniel.

But, in truth, there is not one of the other five judges who concurred with the Chief-Justice and Judges Wayne and Daniel on either of the above points.

Judge Nelson expressly avoided giving any opinion upon them. Indeed, he seems to have leaned to the opinion, that the plea in abatement was not before him : but, after saying there may be some question on this point in the Courts of the United States, he goes on to say, " In the view we [I] have taken of this case, it will not be necessary to pass upon this question ; and we [I] shall therefore proceed at once to an examination of *the case upon its merits.*" He then proceeds to decide the case upon the merits, upon the ground, that, even if Scott was carried into a region where slavery did not exist, his return to Missouri, under the decisions of that State, is to be regarded as restoring the condition of servitude. Judge Nelson has never given the opinion that a negro cannot be a citizen, or that the Missouri Compromise was unconstitutional, or given the least countenance to either of these positions.

Judge Grier, after saying that he concurred with Judge Nelson on the question embraced by his opinion, also said that he concurred with the Chief-Justice that the Missouri-Compromise Act was unconstitutional. He neither expressed the opinion that a negro cannot be a citizen, nor did he intimate that he concurred in that part of the opinion of the Chief-Justice : on the contrary, he placed his concurrence in the *disposal of the case*, as ordered by the Court, expressly upon the ground that the plaintiff was a *slave*, as alleged in the pleas in bar.

Judge Campbell took great pains to avoid expressing the opinion that a free negro cannot be a citizen, and has given no countenance whatever to that dogma. He said, at the commencement of his opinion, after reciting the pleadings, " My opinion in this case is not affected by the plea to the jurisdiction, *and I shall not discuss the question it suggests.*" Accordingly, in an elaborate opinion of more than twenty-five pages 8vo, he confines himself exclusively to the question, whether the plaintiff was a *slave ;* and he adopts or concurs in none of the reasoning of the Chief-Justice, except so far as it bears upon the evidence which shows that the plaintiff was in that condition when he brought his suit. He concurred with the rest of the Court in nothing but the *judgment ;* which was, that the case should be dismissed from the Court below for want of jurisdiction ; and that want of jurisdiction, he takes good care to show, depends, in his view, on the fact that the plaintiff was a *slave*, and not on the fact that he was a free negro, of African descent, whose *ancestors* were slaves.

Thus there were only three of the judges who declared that a free negro, of African descent, whose ancestors were slaves, cannot be a " citizen," for the purpose of suing in the Courts of the United States, and whose opinions on this point are to be regarded as *judicial*, because they were given under the accompanying opinion, that the question was brought before them on the record. As *three* is not a majority of *nine*, the case of Dred Scott does not furnish a judicial precedent or judicial decision on this question.

With regard to the other question in the case, — that arising on what has been called the merits, — the reader will seek an answer to the following questions : —

I. Of the judges who held that the plea in abatement was rightly before them, and that it showed a want of jurisdiction in the Circuit Court, how many went on, notwithstanding their declared opinion that the case ought to have been dismissed by the Circuit Court for that want of jurisdiction, to consider and pass upon the merits which involved the question of the constitutional validity of the Missouri Compromise ?

Answer. — Three : Chief-Justice, and Judges Wayne and Daniel.

II. Of the above three judges, how many held the Missouri-Compromise Act unconstitutional ?

Answer. — Three : the same number and the same judges.

III. Of the judges who did not hold that the question of jurisdiction was to be examined and passed upon, and gave no opinion upon it, how many expressed the opinion on the merits that the Compromise Act was void ?

Answer. — Three : Judges Grier, Catron, and Campbell.

IV. Of the remaining three judges, how many gave no opinion upon either of the two great questions, — that of citizenship, or that of the validity of the Compromise ?

Answer. — One : Judge Nelson.

V. Of the remaining two judges, how many, who held that the question of citizenship was not open, still expressed an opinion upon it in favor of the plaintiff, and *also* sustained the validity of the Compromise ?

Answer. — One : Judge McLean.

VI. The remaining judge (Curtis) held that the question of citizenship was open upon the record ; that the plaintiff, for all that appeared in the plea in abatement, was a citizen ; and, consequently, that the Circuit Court had jurisdiction. This brought him necessarily and judicially to a decision of the merits, on which he held that the Compromise Act was valid.

Thus it appears that six of the nine judges expressed the opinion that the Compromise Act was unconstitutional. But, in order to determine whether this concurrence of six in that opinion constitutes a judicial decision or precedent, it is necessary to see how the majority is formed. Three of these judges, as we have seen, held that the Circuit Court had no jurisdiction of the case, and ought to have dismissed it, because the plea in abatement showed that the plaintiff was not a citizen ; and yet, when the Circuit Court had erroneously decided this question in favor of the plaintiff, and had ordered the defendant to plead to the merits, and, after such plea, judgment on the merits had been given against the plaintiff, and he had brought the record into the Supreme Court, these three judges appear to have held that they could not only decide *judicially* that the Circuit Court was entirely without jurisdiction in the case, but could also give a *judicial* decision on the merits. This presents a very grave question, which goes to the foundation of this case as a precedent or authoritative decision on the constitutional validity of the Missouri-Compromise Act, or any similar law.

If it be true, that a majority of the Judges of the Supreme Court can render a judgment ordering a case to be remanded to a Circuit Court, and there to be dismissed for a want of jurisdiction, which three of that majority declare was apparent on a plea in abatement, and these three can yet go on in the same breath to decide a question involved in a subsequent plea to the merits, then this case of Dred Scott is a judicial precedent against the validity of the Missouri Compromise. But if, on the other hand, the judicial function of each judge who held that the Circuit Court was without jurisdiction, for reasons appearing in a plea to the jurisdiction, was discharged as soon as he had announced that conclusion, and given his voice for a dismissal of the case on that ground, then all that he said on the question involved in the merits was extra-judicial, and the so-called "decision" is no precedent. Whenever, therefore, this case of Dred Scott is cited hereafter in the Supreme Court as a judicial decision of the point that Congress cannot prohibit slavery in a Territory, the first thing that the Court will have to do will be to consider and decide the serious question, whether they have made, or could make, a judicial decision that is to be treated as a precedent, by declaring opinions on a question involved in the merits of a judgment, after they had declared that the Court which gave the judgment had no jurisdiction in the case.

When it is claimed, therefore, in grave State-papers or elsewhere, whether in high or low places, that the Supreme Court of the United States, or a majority of its judges, has authoritatively decided that Congress cannot prohibit slavery in a Territory, it is forgotten or overlooked, that one thing more remains to be debated and determined; namely, whether the opinions that have been promulgated from that Bench adverse to the power of Congress do, in truth and in law, constitute, under the circumstances of this record, an actual, authoritative, judicial decision.

These observations respecting the Dred Scott case are submitted to the public, and especially to the legal profession, with the most entire respect for the several judges; with every one of whom, the writer believes he may say, he has the honor to sustain friendly relations, as he certainly reverences their exalted functions. In perfect consistency with these sentiments, he may be permitted to say, that whatever may be thought of the expediency of expressing opinions on every question brought up by a record, or argued at the bar, there must always be a subsequent inquiry how far such opinions, in the technical posture of the case, as it was presented and disposed of, make a *judicial decision.*

B.

Note on the Property View of Slavery, under the Constitution of the United States.

It is difficult to appreciate the importance which some Southern men appear to attach to the doctrine, that the Constitution of the United States recognizes slaves as *property*. It is a doctrine which cannot increase, by one jot or tittle, the security of the master's right. That right depends exclusively upon the law of the State, and is no more capable of being affected by the Federal Government, when the Federal Constitution is not held to recognize it as a right of property, than it is when the property doctrine is admitted. In point of truth, the Federal Constitution takes notice of the existence of the *status* of slavery in three modes only. *First*, it secures to the federal authority, through the commercial power, the right to prevent the increase of persons in the condition of servitude by *importation*; and there, in this direction, it stops, leaving it entirely to each State to permit their increase by birth upon the soil of the State. *Secondly*, the Constitution recognizes the fact, that besides the "free persons, including those bound to service for a term of years, and excluding Indians not taxed," there may be in the States "other persons;" it permits each State, in making the basis of its Congressional representation, to add to its free population three-fifths of these "other persons;" and, as it is perfectly well known historically that this provision had reference to persons in the condition of servitude, it is quite legitimate to say that the Constitution, through this provision, recognizes such servitude as an existing *status* of persons under the local law. *Thirdly*, the Constitution requires that "persons owing service" in one State, and escaping into another, shall not be discharged of their service in consequence of any law of the State into which they may have escaped, but shall be delivered up.

Now, what is there, in all this, which looks like a recognition of the right of the master as a right of *property*, in the sense in which that term must be used by jurists? The Constitution neither defines, affects, nor deals with, the right itself. If it is the pleasure of the State to abolish it, those who were its subjects pass out of the scope of these provisions of the Federal Constitution. If the State chooses to continue its sanction of the condition of servitude, these provisions continue to operate: they continue to operate so long as there are persons who come within the description, whether the State treats them as persons or as property, or as both. Indeed, under the provision relating to fugitives from service, there is no pretence to say that the Constitution looks to any *property*; for its terms embrace apprentices as well as slaves.

It is of some consequence to the harmonious working of our complex system of government, that the exclusive and irresponsible control of each State
over the personal condition of its inhabitants should not be felt to be capable
of being affected by any theory respecting the mode in which the Federal
Constitution recognizes the peculiarities of that condition.   Of course, no
Slave State can ever permit its sovereign control over its inhabitants to be
put for a moment in peril; not only because its peace and safety require a
jealous defence of its own prerogative, but because that prerogative affords
the only means by which we can rationally hope for a gradual amelioration
of the condition of the African race.   It scarcely seems desirable, therefore, to
weaken the just foundations of this most important right, by maintaining
theories which are in no way necessary to its defence.

With regard to this property doctrine, as affording the means of securing
to slaveholders an entrance into the Territories with their slaves, we are
entirely unable to perceive its value.   It will be conceded by every reflecting
person, that, when the right so to enter the Territories is established, it is a
mere abstraction; and that, unless some means of protecting and upholding
the relation of master and slave are provided under the local law, the relation
will practically cease to exist.   It is equally apparent that such protection
can only be obtained by legislation, either Congressional or Territorial.   If
we suppose the application for a slave code to be made to Congress, how is
the case strengthened by the property doctrine?   If the property carried into
a Territory is of such a character as to require the protection of a peculiar
code, it is of very little consequence whether we call it property before it
arrives, or call it something else; for, until the code is furnished, the thing
itself is of no value.   Whether the necessary code shall or shall not be furnished, depends entirely upon the legislative discretion of Congress.   As the
appeal must be made to that discretion, it would seem to be far better to
have the whole matter depend at once upon those large considerations of
political expediency which should in the end govern it, rather than to under-
take to control the legislative discretion by an artificial subtlety, which sup-
poses a duty to do that which the legislative power cannot be compelled
to do.